Love Twelve Miles Long

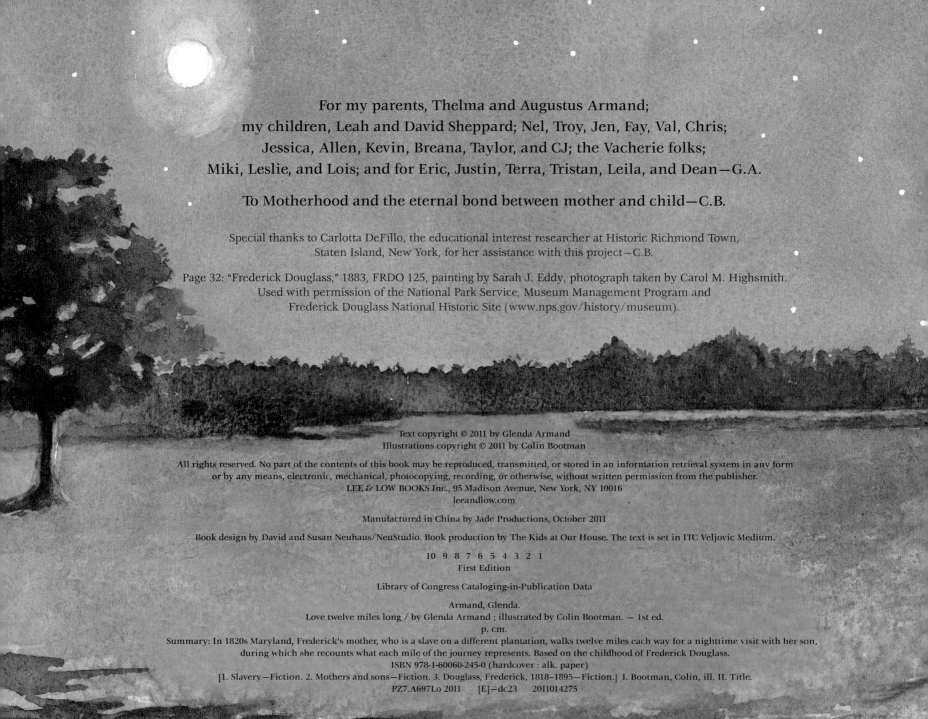

For my parents, Thelma and Augustus Armand;
my children, Leah and David Sheppard; Nel, Troy, Jen, Fay, Val, Chris;
Jessica, Allen, Kevin, Breana, Taylor, and CJ; the Vacherie folks;
Miki, Leslie, and Lois; and for Eric, Justin, Terra, Tristan, Leila, and Dean—G.A.

To Motherhood and the eternal bond between mother and child—C.B.

Special thanks to Carlotta DeFillo, the educational interest researcher at Historic Richmond Town,
Staten Island, New York, for her assistance with this project—C.B.

Page 32: "Frederick Douglass," 1883, FRDO 125, painting by Sarah J. Eddy, photograph taken by Carol M. Highsmith.
Used with permission of the National Park Service, Museum Management Program and
Frederick Douglass National Historic Site (www.nps.gov/history/museum).

LEE & LOW BOOKS Inc., 95 Madison Avenue, New York, NY 10016
leeandlow.com

Manufactured in China by Jade Productions, October 2011

Book design by David and Susan Neuhaus/NeuStudio. Book production by The Kids at Our House. The text is set in ITC Veljovic Medium.

10 9 8 7 6 5 4 3 2 1
First Edition

Library of Congress Cataloging-in-Publication Data

Armand, Glenda.
Love twelve miles long / by Glenda Armand ; illustrated by Colin Bootman. — 1st ed.
p. cm.
Summary: In 1820s Maryland, Frederick's mother, who is a slave on a different plantation, walks twelve miles each way for a nighttime visit with her son,
during which she recounts what each mile of the journey represents. Based on the childhood of Frederick Douglass.
ISBN 978-1-60060-245-0 (hardcover : alk. paper)
[1. Slavery—Fiction. 2. Mothers and sons—Fiction. 3. Douglass, Frederick, 1818–1895—Fiction.] I. Bootman, Colin, ill. II. Title.
PZ7.A697Lo 2011   [E]—dc23   2011014275

Love Twelve Miles Long

by Glenda Armand • Illustrated by Colin Bootman

Lee & Low Books Inc.
New York

This was a special night. Mama had come to visit, and Frederick's stomach was full of the sweet ginger cake she had brought him. As Frederick sat on his mama's lap, her warmth and the sound of her singing filled the candlelit kitchen.

Frederick thought about how happy he had been when he lived with Mama and Grandmama Betsey. Now he lived far away from them in Old Master's house, where the cook, mean old Aunt Katy, took care of him.

When his mama stopped singing, Frederick asked as he always did, "Mama, why can't I live with you?"

"I wish you could live with me, Frederick," Mama said. "But you know I can't look after you while I work in the cornfields all day long."

"Can I come visit you?" asked Frederick.

"No, Child. It's too far away."

"How far?" he asked.

"Twelve miles."

"But you walked here, Mama."

"Oh, it's not far for me," she said. "The way I walk makes the journey shorter."

"Tell me how you walk, Mama. Tell me how you make it shorter."

Frederick looked at Mama. Her eyes reflected the candlelight as she smiled at her son.

"Every mile is special, Frederick. Each mile is for something different."

Now came Frederick's favorite part.

"What's the first mile for?" he asked.

"That's when I do my forgetting," Mama answered.

"What do you forget?"

"I forget how tired I am. I forget that my back hurts and my hands and feet ache. I forget that I've worked all day and have to be in the fields again at sunup. And when the forgetting is done, I start remembering. That's what the second mile is for."

"What do you remember on the second mile?" Frederick asked.

"I remember you, Frederick. I remember how you like to chase squirrels. I remember how you can eat. I remember how you like to ask questions!"

Frederick laughed, and Mama pulled him closer. "I remember how happy I am that you are my son," she added.

Frederick sat up and stuck out his chest. "I am Harriet Bailey's son!"

"Remember that when Aunt Katy is unkind to you," Mama said quietly. She looked up as she heard Aunt Katy stirring in the loft above the kitchen.

"What else do you remember, Mama?" Frederick asked.

"I remember to listen," Mama said.

"Is that what the third mile is for?" Frederick asked.

"Yes," said Mama, "for listening to the sounds of the night."

"What do you hear, Mama?"

"I hear crickets chirping and owls hooting and animals rustling in the trees."

"Can you understand them?"

"Yes, Frederick." Mama spoke just above a whisper. "When I listen to the night sounds, what I hear is 'Look up, Harriet. Look up.'"

"Looking up—that's what the fourth mile is for," Frederick said.

Mama nodded. "For looking up and seeing the stars."

"How many stars, Mama?"

"Too many to count. Sometimes I can see them all spread out before me. Sometimes they wink at me, one by one, through the treetops. I look up at

"What do you wonder about?" asked Frederick.

"I spend the fifth mile wondering about God, this God who made the stars and the animals and you and me. . . ."

"Mama?"

"Yes, Frederick?"

"Why did God make us slaves?"

"God didn't make us slaves, Frederick. We are all God's children. A better day is coming."

"How do you know?" Frederick asked.

"Because I pray," she answered.

"You spend the sixth mile praying," said Frederick, folding his hands. "I know how to pray, Mama. Uncle Isaac taught me the Lord's Prayer."

"Uncle Isaac taught me that prayer too when I was a child. He is a wise old man. Born in Africa."

"Where is Africa?" Frederick asked.

"Far away," said Mama.

"Too far to walk?"

"Yes. Even for me!" Mama said, chuckling. "It's across the wide ocean."

"How wide is the ocean?" asked Frederick.

"Too wide to measure."

"Are the people in Africa free?"

"They are free, but life is hard even in Africa. When you're free, though, you don't mind hard work. That's what I pray for, Frederick. I pray that one day we will all be free. And all that praying makes me feel like singing."

"The seventh mile is for singing!" Frederick said. "What do you sing, Mama? Sad songs or happy ones?"

"I sing whatever my heart feels," Mama replied. "The singing lightens my soul whether the songs be happy or sad. And when my soul is light, I'm ready to walk the eighth mile."

"What's the eighth mile for?" Frederick asked.

"For smiling. I think about happy things. I think about good times."

"What good times, Mama?"

"Oh, like corn-shucking time when we go around from farm to farm helping one another with the harvest. We see which team can shuck the fastest and build the biggest mountain of corn. You never saw corn piled so high in your life!"

"How high?" asked Frederick.

"Too high to measure," Mama said. "It's work, but it's also a time for sharing our burden, and for laughing and joking! Then, after the work is done, there's plenty of eating and dancing."

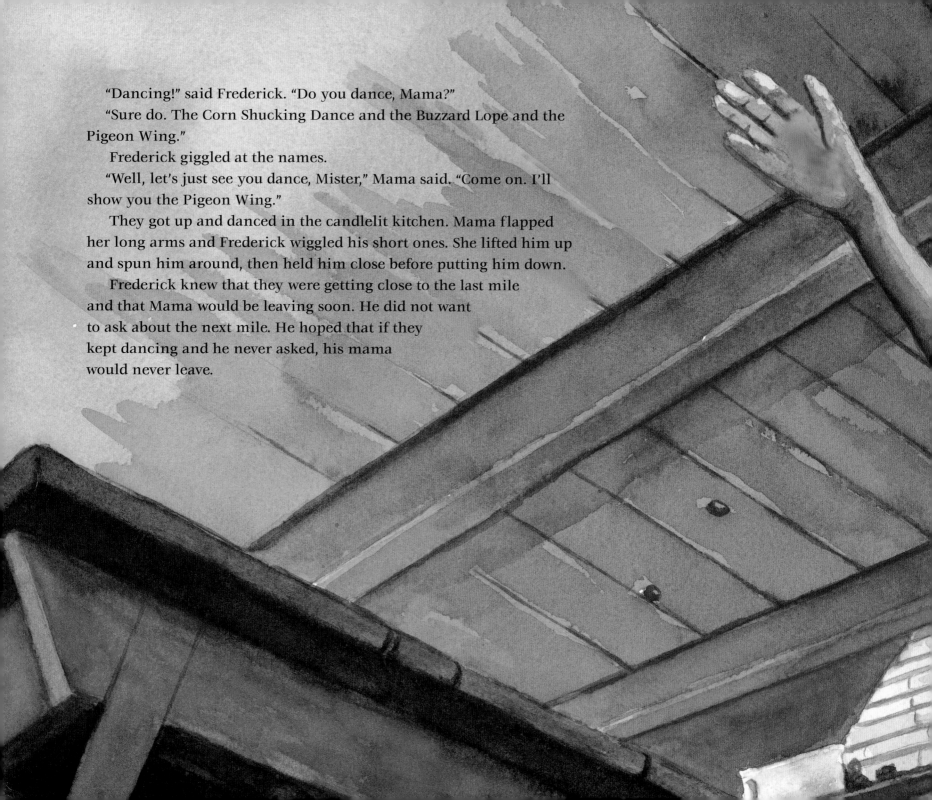

"Dancing!" said Frederick. "Do you dance, Mama?"

"Sure do. The Corn Shucking Dance and the Buzzard Lope and the Pigeon Wing."

Frederick giggled at the names.

"Well, let's just see you dance, Mister," Mama said. "Come on. I'll show you the Pigeon Wing."

They got up and danced in the candlelit kitchen. Mama flapped her long arms and Frederick wiggled his short ones. She lifted him up and spun him around, then held him close before putting him down.

Frederick knew that they were getting close to the last mile and that Mama would be leaving soon. He did not want to ask about the next mile. He hoped that if they kept dancing and he never asked, his mama would never leave.

As Mama led him back to their chair, she asked gently, "Do you know what the ninth mile is for, Frederick?"

"It's for giving thanks."

"That's right. I thank God for giving me life and for being healthy enough to walk here. I thank God for you, Frederick. You give me hope."

"Is the tenth mile for hoping?"

"Yes, Frederick. I have great hope for you. I have hope that one day we will live together as a family. When we're free."

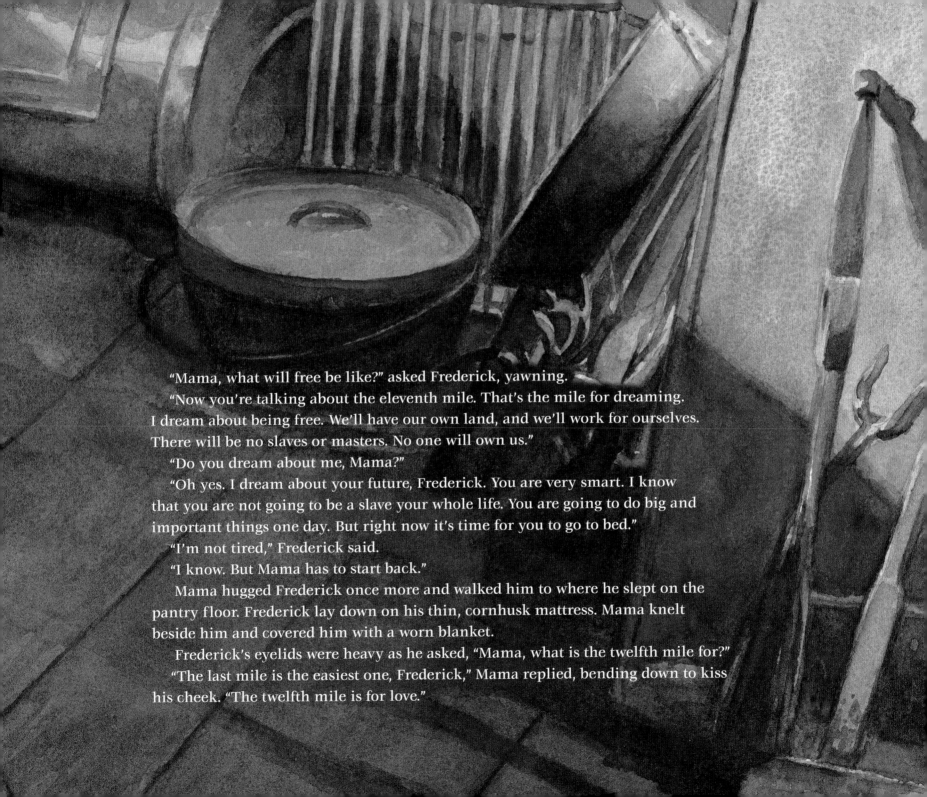

"Mama, what will free be like?" asked Frederick, yawning.

"Now you're talking about the eleventh mile. That's the mile for dreaming. I dream about being free. We'll have our own land, and we'll work for ourselves. There will be no slaves or masters. No one will own us."

"Do you dream about me, Mama?"

"Oh yes. I dream about your future, Frederick. You are very smart. I know that you are not going to be a slave your whole life. You are going to do big and important things one day. But right now it's time for you to go to bed."

"I'm not tired," Frederick said.

"I know. But Mama has to start back."

Mama hugged Frederick once more and walked him to where he slept on the pantry floor. Frederick lay down on his thin, cornhusk mattress. Mama knelt beside him and covered him with a worn blanket.

Frederick's eyelids were heavy as he asked, "Mama, what is the twelfth mile for?"

"The last mile is the easiest one, Frederick," Mama replied, bending down to kiss his cheek. "The twelfth mile is for love."

By the time Mama slipped out into the moonlit night, Frederick was asleep.

When he woke up early the next morning, Frederick ran outside and looked down the road he knew Mama had walked. Through his sadness he could still feel his mama's presence. He thought about all the things she had said.

Mama had told him that there were things he could not count or measure: there were too many stars, the ocean was too wide, and mountains of corn were too high. But there was one thing he could measure. Frederick knew with all his heart that his mama's love was twelve miles long.

Afterword

FREDERICK did gain his freedom, just as his mother had hoped. After escaping from slavery, he changed his last name from Bailey to Douglass to make it harder for his former master to find him. Frederick Douglass eventually led other slaves to freedom and became a famous writer and public speaker who spoke out against slavery. He visited the White House several times to speak with President Abraham Lincoln about freedom for those who were enslaved. When slavery finally ended, Douglass joined the fight for the rights of women.

Although Douglass's mother did not live to see her son become a man, he knew that she would have been proud of him. He said that he owed much of his success to her. Unlike most slaves, Harriet Bailey could read. She may have learned the way Douglass did: from members of their master's family. Harriet Bailey also had a way with words, a gift she passed on to her son, perhaps during those precious nighttime visits. In his autobiography, Douglass wrote that his mother taught him a powerful lesson: that he was not "only a child but somebody's child." Her love for him gave Frederick Douglass the confidence to believe that he was not born to be a slave but was indeed destined to do great things and lead a remarkable life. ❧

Photo courtesy of National Park Service, Museum Management Program and Frederick Douglass National Historic Site.